LIFE LESSONS
unplugged

A Comprehensive Guide to Crucial Like Skills required in today's world

DR. KIRANPREET KAUR

BlueRose ONE.com
Stories Matter
NewDelhi • London

BLUEROSE PUBLISHERS
India | U.K.

BlueRose ONE.com
Stories Matter
New Delhi • London

For permissions requests or inquiries regarding this publication, please contact:

BLUEROSE PUBLISHERS
www.BlueRoseONE.com
info@bluerosepublishers.com
+91 8882 898 898
+4407342408967

ISBN: 978-93-5989-257-3

Cover design: Shubham Verma
Typesetting: Sagar

First Edition: March 2025

This book is an Ode to my loving & supportive Parents
who laid a strong foundation by providing
an understanding, enriching and happy childhood!

Foreword

Dr. Kiranpreet Kaur's Life Lessons Unplugged is a self-help guide focusing on 21 crucial life skills for personal growth, resilience, and success. Aimed at young adults, the book emphasizes self-dependence, courage, and risk-taking to build confidence and emotional strength.

Key lessons include planning life with clear goals, cultivating patience and resilience, and developing self-respect. The book highlights the importance of gratitude, humility, and maintaining mental balance while embracing challenges as opportunities for growth. It stresses continuous self-improvement, nurturing relationships, and adding value to other's lives.

Through personal experiences and motivational insights, Kaur encourages readers to overcome setbacks, stay focused, and lead a fulfilling life. The book serves as a practical manual for developing a strong mindset, empowering individuals to navigate life's uncertainties with confidence, faith, and perseverance.

Kaur's book promises to deliver meaningful lessons for future generations in today's technology driven environment. Indeed, the USP is Kaur shares not just the ideas, but the very principles she lives by...

R.R. Aiyer,

Ex. Executive Senior Vice President,

Amity University Press,

Amity University, Noida.

Introduction

The inspiration to write a book came from the adventures of my own life. A life which was totally different from the plan made and the irony is that Plan B was never thought of. So as the life's picture started rolling, so does the life lessons started unfolding. To handle such an adventurous life, certain life skills came handy. Few of them were already mastered during the college, hostel and working days of life's beautiful phase. But the major ones were learnt during the trying times only.

As being a Personal Impact Coach & Parenting Expert, practicing for over 2 decades, I learnt that the present generation misses some major life skills, which is leading to increase in cases of suicide, low self – esteem and ever dropping ability to bounce back when life hits hard. Young generation is majorly made of fragile ego and over confidence, which gets shattered easily on slightest disappointment from their imagined life.

I hope this book acts as a manual, which they can always consult and connect the dots to a better problem solving. These twenty-one points can help one create their own definition of success, work towards it and have a satisfying beautiful twenties &

THEREAFTER!

Table of Contents

1.

Plan for your Life always

> ***"Give me six hours to chop down a tree and I will spend the first four sharpening the axe."***
>
> ***– Abraham Lincoln***

That is how simply the importance of planning is emphasized to assure progress and growth in life. Whenever I get an opportunity to interact with young people especially teenagers and young adults, I try and help them understand the importance of having a plan for their life. We generally keep on asking young minds, what's your Aim in life? Every child will not be able to frame an answer to this imaginative thought which holds its complete identity in future. So as caregivers it's our duty to help them understand the importance of creating small achievable goals and the satisfaction that they will receive when they achieve these small set goals. Then slowly and steadily push them to look for the activities plan basic things of your trip. From planning a birthday party to planning a wedding - A plan acts more like a map, which will help you in tracking your path & progress. So always try to dream for a bright future to focus and work hard enough in your present.

Planning in your teens and early 20's of how you want to lead your life; your career, marriage etc. would definitely lead you there, **even if not exactly according to the plan but to the nearby safe destination.**

Possessing a professional degree is one of the products of better planning and decision making. Invest some of your time, effort & money to take a professional degree for sure. A professional degree will always tend to sail you through life, professionally as well as personally. A professional degree gives you the much needed confidence, security and at times a VISION as well.

"If you are failing to plan, you are planning to fail."
– Tariq Siddique

Most importantly, Planning gives you the power to define your own needs and therefore the ability to say no to so many distractions which come in your way – just because of your well chalked plan.

A good plan is actually the backbone of success along with some determination to follow the planned path and track one's progress. So always plan and plan well!

"Good fortune is what happens when opportunity meets with planning."
– Thomas Edison

2.

Becoming Self – dependent in all areas of life

"The only person you are destined to become is the person you decide to be."

– Ralph Waldo Emerson

The word 'Self-dependent' puts the whole onus on oneself. It gives immense power to our own being and generates the feeling that the whole universe resides within us. If you don't believe my words, then try it yourself. Close your eyes and now start imagining the power just using this word 'self-dependent' in different areas of your life gives you – how it makes you feel. Imagine you being self-dependent financially, emotionally, mentally, physically. The moment you feel being self –dependent in any of these areas, you feel a sense of power and a sense of responsibility at the same time to use this power. Imagine you being self-dependent physically –

now you will try to frame a fit picture of yourself, then you will try to achieve it because now you understand that you are the only one who is responsible for it, and you have no one to blame for. Your fitness, your independence in daily chores; driving, swimming, doing your technology related works is all in your hands and there is no one else involved.

"The most common way people give up their power is by thinking they don't have any."

– Alice Walker

Once you understand this power, then make sure that you don't let anyone enter in your space of decision making and making it clear to yourself and your loved ones, that I take full onus of my actions and decisions. Then just start taking the required steps of making that area of your life 'self-dependent'.

Self-dependence is the best way to feel freedom in the true sense. You are responsible for your actions, words, deeds. It just gives us the power to break the vicious cycle of blame game in our lives. We start taking steps in the direction of our dreams and start visualizing our success in that area of life. We start believing and behaving in a manner that the failures are ours and so does the successes.

'We spend too much time waiting for others to be for us, what we should be for ourselves!'

Expectations should always be from oneself only and not from others.

From learning to drive, to learning how to cook your favorite delicacies, knowledge about banking and finance, then to become technology friendly e.g. leaning basic computer languages, about different apps other than Instagram/Facebook, handling minor electricity related issues for instance changing bulb, tube etc. gives you immense power and exerts control over various situations.

Financial independence is the most crucial part of self – dependence as it gives you extreme sense of freedom to exercise your decision-making power in all areas of your life. And it gives you the desired respect to begin with and then off course to maintain that level of respect afterwards, you need to be strong on other various values and skills as well like your humility, integrity, behaviour, kindness, courtesy and helpfulness.

It's mandatory to keep reminding yourself that; 'the best day of your life is the one on which you decide your life is your own. There should be no apologies and no excuses. No one to lean on, rely on, or blame. This gift of life is yours solely – it's an amazing journey and you alone are responsible for the quality of it.'

"The greatest thing in the world is to know how to belong to oneself."

– Michel de Montaigne

Self-dependence leads to personal growth and development. When we learn to rely on ourselves instead of others, we develop confidence in ourselves and gain self – esteem. We get a sense of accomplishment as we learn lessons from our falls, mistakes and decisions which went wrong.

"The Best Bet is to Bet on Yourself."

– Arnold Glasow

3.

Taking some well thought of Risks in life leads to a regret free life

"The biggest risk is not taking any risk … In a world that is changing really quickly; the only strategy that is guaranteed to fail is not taking risks."

– Mark Zuckerberg

'Risk something to Gain something' – this is the fundamental rule for growth. In our life we all should definitely take some well-thought of and if possible well calculated risks. Risk taking involves one's willingness and capability to take decisions and related actions which involve high level of uncertainty and equal possibility of profit and loss. But still taking the well analyzed risks to which one is ready to dwell in fully and completely.

From trying a new haircut to trying a new business trick, everything and everywhere involves some amount of risk.

I don't mean risks like gambling here. But surely taking no risks makes one's life a regular one ---

'Means makes 'Johny' a boring boy!!!'

Risks bring newness and new energy. Risk taking helps in developing a sense of responsibility – taking full onus of one's actions! Breaking the shackles of comfort zone is crucial to risk taking and which actually make or break the further opportunities of growth.

Any kind of growth requires risk. Taking risk opens the door of possibilities and can give one a big leap in ones chosen path. A person's true evolution involves some form of risk taking and those well calculated risks hold the hidden gems which take you to the next level in your life – personally as well as professionally. Risk lets us or in fact pushes us to move out of our comfort zone.

'Risk is like that cave which you fear to enter the most, but the fact is that cave holds all the treasure that you are seeking!'

You are one decision away from a completely different life. And that decision needs you to vouch something out there and to fight with your fear. But still never be afraid to try something new. Life gets boring when you stay within the limits of what you already know.

'There is no shame in making mistakes or goof-ups, while trying to figure things out. The purpose is to live a fulfilling life and not a perfect life!'

When I elaborate the word RISKS; every letter signifies the importance of risks and the change that risks bring in our lives!

RISKS – Rise Incredibly in Situations that Knock us Somewhere.

My **life challenged me many times but the deal or to say trick is to challenge life back.** Losing pregnancy weight of 32 kgs, dealing with a 7th month miscarriage or going to Mrs. India … Every time life was giving me challenges and I was challenging life back in my own way by giving 100% in overcoming all challenges.

"If you take plenty of well thought risks in life; you will surely have plenty of memories to cherish and stories to share."

I believe the fears we don't face upfront becomes our limiting beliefs. These fears always put limits in front of us whenever we are trying to achieve something new. These limits are created from our past experiences. We need to face our fears to break these limits and barriers. Fear of failure stops us from taking risks in life, but that fear & doubt need to be pushed away and should be replaced with faith and logical reasoning. Once taken, complete surrender to it assures your 100% input to it. There is never a guarantee that the risks taken, will take you to an accelerated path. But one thing I know for sure that if given 100% to the risk involving task, you will surely not regret as you will for sure reach the next level in life with the life lessons which will make you wiser and technically speaking more equipped to handle life's tricky situations next time!

That's why I always want to emphasize that Risk taking is not bad if it covers two aspects. One that risk should always be well thought of; the pros and cons are evaluated well in time and secondly, once the risk has been taken, one should now give their 100% to it – fully & completely!!

'You will never change unless the pain of remaining the same is greater than the change itself!'

The 3 C's in life or so to say the 3 powers we possess as humans should be well exercised in life:

"Choice, Chance, Change"

It's our Choice to;

GIVE UP, GIVE IN or GIVE IT ALL, to our chosen path!!

You must make a **choice**, to take the required **chance** if you want anything to **change** in your life! Don't wait for the perfect moment – just create it. Whether it's a new habit, a big goal, or a shift in mindset, you need to take that chance, that risk, that leap, to bring that big change in life.

"Everybody fails; it's no big deal.
It's what being human is.
Don't let that stop you from taking risks."

–Katty Kay

4.

Never Underestimate the Power of Courage

"Courage is the commitment to begin without any guarantee of success."
– Johann Wolfgang Von Goethe

What does risk-taking requires the most?

It's COURAGE.

Courage is most crucial and center of being independent in life. One of the biggest lessons life taught me in my tough times was to be courageous. In a world full of uncertainties and fearful situations, courage is the quality if well developed, keeps us going.

"The will to do, the soul to dare."
– Walter Scott

There are situations in life where fear and doubt accompany us. In such trying times, an affirming voice of courage motivates us to stay on track and believe in ourselves. Courage is our ability to keep moving forward on our planned path despite the fact that the chosen path frightens us.

Always make efforts and take out time to acknowledge and understand your fears, but don't let them dictate your actions. Choose courage and faith over fear.

This cannot be stressed enough that this by far is undeniably the most assuring of all qualities to the road towards a successful and fulfilling life. You know, some days courage means 'holding on' and on other days it simply means 'letting go!'

We may have the best of plans, ideas and strategies required for success, but nothing succeeds till we empower ourselves with the courage to take the required actions. No matter how scary or uncertain the first step may seem, but showing courage is what pushes us on the chosen path.

Be courageous to go for what you want. Being brave enough to challenge the fearful situation in front can never go out of style or so to say, is never an old school act. **Being courageous and brave is always the most 'IN' thing!**

And you know the best part here is that '**Courage is Contagious**' – when your siblings, colleagues, employees see you showing courage and taking steps, they are likely to follow your shown path. Courage creates ripple effect in our lives leading to big transformations, not only in our life but the community at large.

As discussed in previous section, Life is all about risks and risks require Courage. If you don't have the courage to take some risks, you will not get the desires of your heart fulfilled.

From saying I LOVE YOU to saying WE PART WAYS – all needs some courage and involves some risk.

Courage to take the required next step,

Courage to stick to your principles,

Courage to leave the past,

Courage to move on,

Courage in doing something new,

Courage in saying NO –

Your very identity is created by how you view yourself, how much respect and love you possess for yourself. Slowly, this self-created identity starts reflecting in all areas of our lives, in our relationships, career, health, social life!

Leaving those who don't value your relationship, your presence but that so with dignity; is the level of clarity, that self-respect brings to our lives. Never beg for a seat when you can build your own table.

"Don't lose your self-respect in order to gain a relation, as in this process you will lose your whole worth."

When you know your own worth and you respect your own being whole heartedly; you never let anyone cross their limits and disregard you. But **the prerequisite of Self-respect is Self-acceptance.**

"Just being you is actually not that difficult!

It's experiencing freedom in true sense!!"

Accepting yourself – your charm, your flaws, your mistakes with grace helps you create a picture of yourself that you respect and regard.

These are some simple yet profound words of wisdom to be followed completely in life -

If you want others to respect you, it all somewhere begins with you respecting yourself, accepting yourself.

Value yourself because when you undervalue your own worth, you give yourself to the wrong people, things and efforts which always leaves you feeling empty and confused. Always value this fact that you have earned your experience and your past. Be grateful for what makes you, you. Give yourself to ideas and people that make you feel valuable and loved. Acknowledge that you are worth it, you deserve all this love!

'Never chase love, affection or attention. If it isn't given freely by another person, it isn't worth having.'

Accepting oneself begins somewhere with forgiving ourselves for acts which have been done in past and taking yourself gradually towards a regret free zone which takes time and constant effort. **'Forgive yourself to free yourself!'** Accept yourself fully and let go of your harsh internal critic. Unknowingly, we disgrace ourselves by using negative disregardful words about ourselves. Dwelling in self-pity or using harsh words to describe our looks – how can we expect others to respect us!

Believe in yourself always, especially more on the days when no one else believes in you. Believing in yourself is a full-time job and you get no days off.

My philosophy in life in this area has been pretty simple yet amazingly empowering –

"When nobody else celebrates you, learn to celebrate yourself. When nobody compliments you, then compliment yourself. It's not up to other people to keep you encouraged.
It's up to you!
Encouragement should come from inside."

6.

Seize the Day – make every day count when working towards your goals

CARPE DIEM[1]! CARPE DIEM!

Oh, seize the day my dear – make every present moment count!! We always listen to various motivational and spiritual speakers talk about the importance of living in the moment. Most of us today are either stuck in our past or worried about our future. We hardly stay focused in our present day and that's why many of us are not able to make most of the present day we are in.

I have been a procrastinator all through, even before that time when I even understood the word itself. I wanted to do a lot and achieve big things, but whenever started taking steps towards my set goals, I was always engulfed in the

[1] CARPEDIEM in Latin means Seize the day

thoughts of either past or future. Then one day while reading an article I realized the power of taking small steps every day and how it can lead you to achieving your targets sooner or later. It reminded me of the famous story of Tortoise and rabbit from our childhood. The importance of keep moving, taking baby steps but not stopping is of paramount importance.

The realization of the fact that if we make merely 0.1% improvement in our work every day – it culminates to a big number by end of the year and takes us up in our ladder of desired success. James Clear, the famous author of the book, Atomic habits talk about 'the power of tiny gains' - The impact of a 1% improvement in his theory of marginal gains. He talks distinctively about the power of small yet conscious decisions on daily basis shapes our life. Master the art of continuous improvement. Small changes eventually lead to big results. Little by little, a little becomes a lot.

Setting clear intentions for your day and life at large assists you in guiding your thoughts and actions towards your goals and values. **Learn to identify negative thought patterns before they take hold, interrupt them with your conscious awareness and then swapping them with empowering affirmations.**

Everyone is not capable of making big changes overnight and the fact is that I believe that the term 'overnight success' is a myth. It's actually culmination of endless days and nights to become an 'overnight success'. It's like working hard consistently for days, months & years to finally reach at a place where you become an overnight star.

'You plan your actions today, and those actions create your future.'

So when planning to move forward in life always focus on making small yet consistent progress every day. Whether planning to lose weight, writing a book, learning to speak a particular language etc. – focus on working every day, seizing the day and you will reach your desired goals well in time. My entire life revolves around this fact that plan your actions today and those actions eventually create your future.

We always work for a better tomorrow. But when tomorrow comes, instead of enjoying we again think of a better tomorrow. Let's have a better today.

'If you do not use today better than yesterday, then why do you need tomorrow?'

Let's seize the day and daily plan small steps that you can take today that works as an investment. Walk slowly but steadily like 'the tortoise' and you will surely reach your finish point.

> ***"We cannot become what we want to be,***
> ***by remaining what we are!"***
>
> ***Max De Pree***

7.

Having Patience to finish what you have started

> ***"I pray to be like the ocean, with soft currents, maybe waves at time. More and more, I want consistency rather than the highs and lows."***
>
> ***– Drew Barrymore***

This needs will power! There is this word we listen often today and it's considered essential for success – it's 'consistency'. Yes, it is one of the major ingredients in the recipe of success. **'Consistency is what transforms average into excellence.'** But what I want to focus here is that for that consistent action, patience is utmost. Results don't come all of a sudden; normally visibility of results is prominent after a certain gap. Great things take time and you must be willing to be patient throughout your journey. To keep yourself going during this gap period, you need to work on your patience levels which are directly connected to your will-power.

'Be Stronger than your strongest excuse.'

On the road to achievements, there come many highs and many lows, but you keeping your balance, patience and courage in place is what guarantees your growth no matter how slow. **While patience will help you to accept the process, consistency is what brings you desired results. 'Let patience and consistency together be your superpower.'**

Patience is cultivated, like most virtues. It's your secret weapon when wanting to conquer big things. We live in a world where everyone is chasing instant gratification, it's essential to understand that, if you are able to put in work on consistent basis and at the same time remain patient, you will surely win. Dwelling on mistakes, feeling jealous, rushing things won't bring you results any faster. If you accept and understand this fact, stay patient and willingly do necessary work, you will already be ahead of most people in your field.

But please remember, there is a difference in being laid back and being patient. Here during this patience time, you are constantly taking action and not just waiting for things to happen. As long as you are putting in the necessary work and making sure that you are consistent, then the only requirement is patience.

With grace and most of it unknowingly, I always assumed myself as a patient being. In college days, I used to just keep on working and used to find myself achieving my goals organically. But the major realization about my patience levels hit me when I was morally and physically in the low phase of life. During covid, I was going through too much in life. My work was on a halt, body was out of shape and I was lowest on energy, used to feel my life meant kids and house only. There is absolutely nothing wrong with giving yourself completely 'In' for your choices – my kids and subsequently staying at home. But for someone like me , who was always working and going out daily, this was hard to accept, sort of complete lockdown at home with two kids (though it was chosen by me.) Now my patience was at a toss daily, even to maintain a simple routine. Creating a routine for myself for getting up, exercising was a real task which needed consistent efforts to stay consistent. At this already overwhelming phase of life, I took a big decision of starting to study again! After a gap of almost 18 years, starting my 3rd long awaited post-graduation in Management and Human Resource required some courage. Paid the fees in a jiffy, in a very motivated short phase but reality hit hard when the online classes started, assignment deadlines were issued, exams date sheets came out and project submission dates were given! This was really difficult. With an infant and an elementary grade child doing her online classes, it really needed patience and a lot was on my platter. I needed will power to finish what I had started. There were many times when I just thought of leaving it in between. During every semester exams, either I got sick, or kids were sick, or some unseen emergency came up, everyone around also just wanted me to leave it, as I have a lot of other priorities to cope up with. But whenever I used to look at my 9-year-old daughter, I thought to myself, what example I want to draw for her. I always preach her finish what you have started, the painting, the drink, the cycle rounds and so on. And so I kept on taking small steps and moving forward. With this will power, one day at a time, I accomplished what I call my second covid baby: my third post-graduation in management and human resource from a renowned university. This degree along with my past experience eventually helped me to get into many big companies as a corporate coach later.

Always remember that patience and consistency go hand in hand. Patience is that quiet strength which allows us to navigate through challenges and wait for results without losing hope and most importantly constantly taking consistent steps and not stopping while waiting. Keep going even when things don't seem very positive and pleasing. **The actions we take in such tough situations, are the ones we are most proud.** So, get in action mode as soon as possible. It's actually action that creates motivation and not the other way around. For me action is an antidote to my anxiety, and it helps me direct all my energy in achieving my desired goal.

"Small disciplines repeated with consistency every day lead to great achievements gained slowly over time."

– John C. Maxwell

8.

Being Resilient

"Resilience is not about being unbreakable; it's about being able to put the pieces back together and continue on with renewed hope and courage."

The dictionary meaning of resilience is 'the capacity to withstand or to recover quickly from difficulties.' Being resilient is the most crucial of life skills discussed widely in today's world. And remember 'Being Resilient is always a choice, when you choose to rise above your difficulties and become the amazing human you are meant to be."

For me I realized in my twenties only that resilience is going to be my 'armour'. Being a psychology student and passionate about it too, read extensively about it that 'if we don't bring ourselves back from a particular setback in time, then depression is what creeps in soon.'

To be honest with you, resilience was never a much known and experienced skill till my marriage. Let me picture it for you in a fast forward scene, I was a below average student in school and was actually hopeless for life. But after school, something shifted in me and I became a girl who was ready to first take up & then beat challenges. I became and stayed a rank holder till my masters. I was a girl full of laughter and charm which used to attract people towards me like magnets. I started working, went US for further internship and life seemed amazing and future looked heavenly.

But then something out of the bloom came up and next thing I knew I was married and in the most non-cooperative environment. Then is the actual time when I came in real contact and connect with the very word 'resilience' in its true sense.

Being resilient helped me to look for options in every scenario. The scenarios were most of the times very tough but my resilient and 'never give up' attitude helped in making small yet steady and significant marks in my field.

'The comeback is always stronger than the setback.'

I want to pass on this realization that whatever your chosen field is and whichever path you are on, there are going to be bumps. I believe just acknowledge those bumps but at the same time look for what can be done now to have minimum loss. Have you ever heard about the Minimum Loss Principle? This principle simply guide producers how to minimize losses in a particular situation. I have applied this principle in my life thoroughly. Always looking for best that could be done in a particular given situation to minimize loss. And by loss it's never only material loss, but also the fear of losing oneself and one's self-worth.

No matter what you are going through today, do not give up. As long as there is life, there is hope.

"If you can't fly then run, if you can't run then walk, if you can't walk then crawl, but whatever you do you have to keep moving forward."

– Martin Luther King Jr.

9.

Reflect to Reset

"Life can only be understood backwards; but it must be lived forwards."
– Soren Kierkegaard

One thing that's mandatory when assuring a fulfilling and elevated journey on the path of success is Reflection. Reflecting on the decisions made, actions taken and outcomes received should be an ongoing activity, if one plans to progress to the next level in one's life. Reflecting on various highlights, points, mistakes, opportunities which otherwise may have been overlooked and equipping one well in advance to handle the next opportunity that knocks!

Reflecting on the scenario that have just taken place, actually acts like a Reset where one feels more aligned to their goals and better prepared to handle different situations.

'If you don't know what to pursue in life right now, pursue yourself. Pursue becoming the healthiest, happiest, most healed, most present, most confident version of yourself. Then the right path will reveal itself.'

This is your opportunity to recharge, reflect and cultivate a growth mindset. Whether it's practicing mindfulness, diving into a new skill, or simply spending quality time with those you love, every action you take brings you close to your best self.

Always remember to prioritize your growth and healing, the right path will unfold before you.

There are many ways to reflect on your day and reflect on your actions. The ways can be learnt from someone or they can be crafted according to your comfort and what works best for you.

I love to write and for that I maintain a daily journal. I ponder over my day at night and also on my week every Sunday morning. This activity helps me keep track of what's missing and what needs to be adopted for coming week to keep the growth chart upwards.

'Life is like a mirror. It will reflect back to the thinker what he thinks into it.'

Reflecting on the past month and also in end of the year, are one of the rituals I maintain. What I know for sure is that this kind of reflection on your days, definitely help you become a true achiever by becoming a better person. You are able to introspect on your actions and behaviors which are pulling you back or hindering your success and take actions to bring the required changes.

Brian Tracy, one of the most profound writers of our times emphasized on reflection in a beautiful manner by saying;

> ***"It doesn't matter where you are coming from. All that matters is where you are going."***

The biggest lesson here is what matters most is who I am now rather than who I was, and this clarity comes from daily reflection.

Reflection is an amazing skill and should be practiced early in life to gain perspective, learn from your mistakes/experiences and this helps one understand oneself better. Regular practice of reflecting on your day aligns you with your core values and your set goals.

"By three methods we may learn wisdom: First, by reflection, which is noblest; Second, by imitation, which is easiest: and third by experience, which is the bitterest."

- Confucious

10.

Learn to Focus

Focus on present
Focus on goodness
Focus on positivity

"If you must look back, do so forgivingly.
If you must look forward, do so prayerfully.
However, the wisest thing you can do is be present in the present...Gratefully."

– Maya Angelou

Today the world is full of distractions, so learning to focus on life in hand positively seems a major task and it's generally a learned skill. We all have heard a lot about the importance of staying present to the present but when we start implementing it, it seems nearly impossible. So I came up with a trick for myself. I try to make up something which keeps me occupied all the time. My mom's words from childhood have carried immense relevance in my adult life. She always said 'an idle mind is devil's workshop'. That's why, I try never to stay completely idle except my rest periods (btw which are also planned). For me to be fully present in 'now' needs some planning so I know what to do next when I am done with the task in hand. In fact, I believe in planning and adding my rest time to my roughly chalked schedule as well. Here the take is that I don't plan too far, short crisp goals of just the closest times. For this I write my three tasks of the day in morning that need to be accomplished to call it a day and then I am sorted. Like this I have achieved a lot in my career and life. Small wins everyday accumulates to be big success.

"Don't leave anything for later.
Later, the coffee gets cold.
Later, you lose interest.
Later, the day turns into night.
Later, people grow up.
Later, people grow old.
Later, life goes by,
Later, you regret not doing something …
when you had the chance."

-Toshikazu Kawaguchi

We all have been looking for answer to this question:

How to overcome procrastination and boost our productivity?

Here we talk about planning, goals and then all of a sudden about staying in present! How's that even possible?

Yes, we need plans, we need goals to find out what we want to achieve in long run, how we can achieve it. For staying consistent on this journey towards your goals, you need daily tasks and achievements. You need to keep your present fully utilized and achieving.

'The past is in your head but the present is what you have in your hands.'

Developing the skill to focus, is like sharpening your axe. The one who can overcome their distractions and focus well on the task in hand, is already a winner. ***Bruce Lee*** once emphasized this power of focus in our lives by saying;

"The Successful Warrior is the average man, with Laser like Focus."

There is something good in every one's life, we just need to shift our perspective and don't let difficulties fog our glasses and we become unaware of all the things which are going well. For this, the most effective way is maintaining a gratitude journal on daily basis, and it holds the power to bring positivity in light once again.

'When you focus on problems, you will have more problems. But when you focus on possibilities, you will have more opportunities.'

Goodness gives birth to more goodness, and it works as a cycle – goodness brings goodness and kindness brings kindness. **Don't overlook your power to create goodness in this world on your own level.**

"You meet saints everywhere. They can be anywhere. They are people behaving decently in an indecent society."

– Kurt Vonnegut

11.

Cultivating Faith

"When you go deep waters, I will be with you."
– Isaiah 43:2

Faith never lets you fail...whether you win or lose but with faith you always sail through!

This is not just a thought or a quote to put out there but my very experienced feelings. Faith in a supreme power, by whatever name we address it ... exists. Faith that whatever is happening or going to happen is going to land up in my favor eventually always helped me control my anxiety at various difficult unpredictable times of my life.

Whatever is happening is going to happen, no matter how much anxious or stressed we get. But what matters is striving to perform your part perfectly till last and then being ready to accept the result gracefully is your power.

Take sometime out to pray daily and ask for his grace. Prayer is scientifically proven to lower anxiety and creates a sense of calmness and belief that everything will work out.

Pray! Pray without missing. Pray regularly. Prayer acts as a catalyst that can speed up your blessings to come to you on time.

Faith and prayer give you hope and once you choose hope, everything seems possible. Hope is a rope that swings you though life!

"Hope is praying for rain, but faith is bringing an umbrella."

Cultivating faith in a higher power requires intention and then effort. Living a life where you intentionally take out time to sit in silence, mediate, pray and visit your place of worship. It all begins somewhere with these acts but is surely much deeper than this.

We as psychologists, focus a lot on the fact that when feeling low and having negative thoughts, just talk to someone who loves you and understands you and share your feelings and your vulnerability with them and you will feel lighter. But with personal experience and then helping so many people for years, one thing I always emphasize is that when you hit your rock bottom, and you are feeling lonely, the only rescue is your faith in your God. Just sitting in his memory, like literally talking to someone, seeking direction and praying is what helps most in the times of despair and provides a way out. There comes a time in your life when you don't seek physical presence or validation from another human to feel better and yourself again. You start feeling someone always being there to guide you and at your rescue.

I believe the best gift that you can give yourself and your future generations is the foundation of faith and belief in the immense power that faith holds. It helps in clearer decision making, working hard to achieve targets and then at one point surrendering to this higher power and then accepting the results and outcome whatever they are, with full gratitude.

ਤੇਰਾ ਕੀਆ ਮੀਠਾ ਲਾਗੈ ॥

ਹਰਿ ਨਾਮੁ ਪਦਾਰਥੁ ਨਾਨਕੁ ਮਾਂਗੈ ॥੨॥੪੨॥੯੩॥

These lines from Sri Guru Granth Sahib ji has given immense power to me in those challenging times when life seemed out of control and surrendering to the higher power was extremely difficult. But these lines gave me strength and belief that my Waheguru can't do anything bad with me. Whatever has happened has happened for my good and I completely accept his gifts with open heart.

**** Tera Kiya Meetha Laage**
- Guru Arjan Dev in Raag Asa from Sri Guru Granth Sahib ji

ਤੇਰਾ ਕੀਆ ਮੀਠਾ ਲਾਗੈ ॥

तेरा कीआ मीठा लागै ॥
Ŧerā kī▫ā mīṯẖā lāgai.
Your actions seem so sweet to me.

ਹਰਿ ਨਾਮੁ ਪਦਾਰਥੁ ਨਾਨਕੁ ਮਾਂਗੈ ॥੨॥੪੨॥੯੩॥

हरि नामु पदारथु नानकु मांगै ॥२॥४२॥९३॥
Har nām paḏārath Nānak mā'ngai. ||2||42||93||
Nanak begs for the treasure of the Naam, the Name of the Lord. ||2||42||93||

12.

Staying Grateful – Practicing Gratitude

"Gratitude is riches.
Complaint is poverty."
– Doris Day

Focus on what you want more in your life. Stay grateful to attract more reasons to be grateful for! Before I move further on this point, I want to sight an example here which is my favorite when talking about the importance of gratitude in our lives. Always observe around or remember your own childhood, parents always tend to give more and love more to the child who is thankful as compared to the siblings who are cribbing. Parents always feel like giving more to a grateful child than to a cribbing one, same way God / Universe also gives more to a grateful being than to a thankless one!! Therefore, if you want more happiness in your life, the simple trick to attract that is to first become extremely grateful for all the happiness that you already possess.

Expressing Gratitude is difficult at most times but if this followed regularly can provide nourishment to mind, body and soul. Appreciating things in life that are meaningful and hold value to you is a very beautiful practice. Taking some time out to notice and acknowledge the various things that you are grateful for holds the power to boost your mood, feel positivity and brightening your overall outlook towards life.

Being grateful for the small things, the ones which actually doesn't make sense! Being grateful is a powerful and blissful habit but a tough one to develop. For example, just close your eyes and imagine the small blessings or the for - granted people in your life (the easiest and most used example is your parents and helpers) and now imagine these not being physically present anymore, and before you know, your hands will automatically join in gratitude. Once you begin to take note of all the things that you are grateful for, you begin to lose sight of all the things that you lack.

'Practicing Gratitude helps you see what's there instead of what isn't.' Your mind doesn't see them as something to be grateful for as they are always available to you. But at the same time, you don't want to lose them but thanking for them is a real task. Work on developing this 'attitude of gratitude' well in time, as it is the most rewarding habit.

"Happiness cannot be travelled to, owned, earned, worn, or consumed. Happiness is the spiritual experience of living every minute with love, grace and gratitude."

– Denis Waitley

Always remind yourself that being happy doesn't mean you have it all. It simply signifies that you are grateful for all you have. It's reciprocal, where one feels happy because one is grateful. Being grateful is a choice we make; we chose to be grateful for small blessings and then that gratefulness allows us to be happier!

"Gratitude is magnetic; it attracts many more reasons to be grateful for! Practice gratitude!!"

Gratitude is the strongest of all emotions and it has been scientifically proven to improve your brain health and your overall life's quality. If one has to name one simple habit that can boost your overall health and happiness quotient then that would be expressing thanks daily. When you focus on what you are thankful for and what you appreciate in your life, you rewire your brain for joy, peace, and holistic well-being.

Your day should begin and end with gratitude always! This daily practice for gratitude can magically transform our lives. We need to dwell on this simple philosophy that it's not happiness that brings us reason to be grateful for. It's actually gratitude that brings us more happiness.

'If a person could do one simple thing to increase their overall health and happiness then expressing gratitude on a regular basis must be it.'

13.

Stay Grounded – Staying Humble

"It was pride that changed angels into devils: it is humility that makes men as angels."

– Saint Augustine

In a world dominated by social media, false ego and obsession with oneself, the virtue of humility is highly valued. Humility is being modest and having a realistic view of oneself.

Staying grounded and humble can actually give you wings to fly anywhere safely and still you are connected to your roots. While growing up our parents put a lot of emphasis on 'Sanskars'. But generally, the explanation of 'being sanskari' is confined to; listening and obeying elders, behaving in a certain "appropriate" manner, doing 'pairi – pauna' to elders and the definition generally ends here of 'being sanskari'. Meeting & working with teens & youngsters for so many years made me realize that humility as a quality of a good character is far forgone. Checking your Wats up messages and not responding, knowing someone personally but still ignoring them in social gatherings, exchanging pleasantries depending on one's mood on that particular day, dealing with people based upon the number of brands they carry in their attire and social status are some of the characteristic traits of today's generation. We are trying to feel superior by doing such frivolous acts and satisfying a false sense of ego.

3 thumb rules to Remember here;

Ego kills Growth,

Jealousy kills Peace,

And

Anger kills Wisdom.

What I know for sure is that '**Never change your originality for the sake of others**', because no one can play your role better than you. Changing your attitude and behavior depending on how powerful someone seems is the most artificial and superficial trait of one's character. Don't be so easily intimidated with money or material things. A poor man today can become affluent tomorrow. **Change is constant**! So, if you have choice and wit available to you at the right time, choose to stay humble - graceful if you're a woman and gentleman if you are the other half of the globe, no matter what the situation is!

"Humility is the solid foundation of all virtues."
- Confucius

Here when talking about humility, it's absolutely important to understand that there is a prominent distinction between being humble and having low self-esteem. A humble person possesses high self – esteem and has confidence in himself but at the same time they value and respect others and their viewpoints in the same manner. They are empathetic towards other beings and open to change. For a humble person it's never 'my way or highway'. It's always a collaboration and connection which is their main characteristic. My mother used to clearly indicate this importance by quoting; 'it's the coins which make noise, a note is quite because it knows its value very well and the value it creates for others.' Humble people do not boast about their accomplishments and abilities, they don't rub on it. They always try to create value by being present and approachable.

As millennial, Gen Z & Generation Alpha ruling the world right now, we need to continuously and consistently nourish this trait of humility and staying humble throughout our life to make this world a better place to live. Humility exudes self-confidence for sure. A person who believes that he/she is loved and has a sense of confidence in their own self, will always be more humble and more empathetic towards others. Cultivating this trait of humility is necessary if we want to have an everlasting sense of satisfaction, calmness amidst of chaos and peace which we keep on looking for in various wellness & spirituality retreats all over the world later on in our lives. The small conscious acts of kindness and humbleness on daily basis creates an amazing 'aura' around you which makes you look & feel divine without much effort and makes you stand out in a crowd. Aren't we all looking for some form of recognition & appreciation? "What goes around comes around!!"

"Being humble means recognizing that we are not on earth to see how important we can become, but to see how much difference we can make in the lives of others."

- GORDON B. HINCKLEY

14.

Move on in life but take the Lesson along

"Nothing ever goes away until it has taught us what we need to know."
– Pema Chodron

Being aware is the key! **'Lessons in life are repeated until they are learned.'** I truly believe in this line! When some similar incidents keep on happening to you, you need to sit down and look for signals - what are these incidents trying to teach you? Become mindful and observe closely.

'You can learn from history, but you can't live in it.' I always tried to believe and keep my attention to the powerful opportunity that lies underneath each challenge. Setbacks are not failures and obstacles in your growth; they actually act as stepping stones nudging you closer to your wisdom and look for your bigger goal here.

There is a famous Japanese Quote that says,

If you get on the wrong train,

get off at the nearest station.

The longer it takes you to get off,

the more expensive the return trip will be.

Sometimes we keep on doing what's wrong simply because once we took a wrong decision unknowingly and now, we keep on repeating it as we are afraid to take that tough call to back out or leave it. We are afraid what people will say or how your family and friends will respond. Here what's important is how you feel because it's your life which is getting affected at end of the day. Take your lesson and move on in life!

Mr. Ratan Tata had a powerful quote which has always been my driving force on days when I felt deeply affected by people's behavior and actions:

"Take the stones people throw at you and use them to build a monument."

When familiar experiences and people tend to cross my path, I always pause, reflect and ask myself: What's the lesson here? These familiar experiences are actually our opportunities to find our greatest strengths. It's all about looking at these experiences with hidden lessons from a different perspective and embracing them wholeheartedly to unleash your true potential.

> ***"Sometimes good things fall apart so better things can fall together."***
>
> ***– Marilyn Monroe***

Some breakups, some friendships, some relations were not meant to be in your life forever. Instead the lessons they taught were meant to be with you.

'Don't cling to a mistake just because you spent a lot of time making it!'

Moving on in life is essential as staying in past can create toxicity and hence the vicious cycle of hurt and pain goes on. Holding on to pain and hurt is equal to self-abuse. We need to break this cycle and move on towards better options. You can reach your full potential once you move on in life. It encourages growth and development and helps in achieving goals. Moving on creates space for positive change and break the cycle of blame game. It's liberating and helps you evolve. Now you can look for new opportunities and embracing them with open heart. **'Your past has** given you immense strength and wisdom, so isn't it something to celebrate?'

"Holding on is believing that there's only a past;
letting go is knowing that there's a future."
- Daphne Rose Kingma

15.

Pay Attention to what you Feed your Mind - Keep your Thoughts Upbeat and Nourishing

"Your diet is not only what you eat. It's what you watch, what you listen to, what you read, the people you hang around ... be mindful of the things you put into your body emotionally, spiritually and physically."

Be watchful of what and who stays in your mind. Practicing the art of keeping your thoughts upbeat and nourishing is the most precious gift one can give oneself in their whole lifetime. It means we have the intention to take care of ourselves holistically – physically, emotionally and spiritually. Research proves that it's almost impossible to stop thoughts from coming. There are times when no negative thought is bothering us but some random thought about an uncertainty or some event in future makes us anxious. So here is the trick which always worked with me, 'to trick the mind by diverting it; replacing the unwanted thought with the wanted one.'

In fact, this trick worked with a lot of my clients over the years and gave them confidence that they can manage and direct their thoughts, and they are not slaves of their thoughts.

In routine life, when things are going topsy-turvy especially at that time, keeping a track of your thoughts can be a game changer. Don't let your thoughts go haywire in the initial stages only. Train your mind to acknowledge the thought and then let it pass at the first place, especially if it is a thought which makes you feel short or degrade you, should never be entertained. Like other qualities, this also is cultivated and practiced over time. Just get into the habit of holding onto upbeat and uplifting thoughts if eventually you want to feel blessed with a nourished mind.

What you watch, listen to, read, and the people you surround yourself with will impact your brain and your potential. Be mindful of what you consume emotionally, spiritually, and physically. Every input shapes your growth, learning and performance. Choose wisely.

We all try our best to avoid medicine (popping a pill every time) to stay healthy, right? The magic word is 'immunity'. Work towards improving your immunity against all kinds of negativity. But you know, medicines and immunity are not always found in bottles, tablets or vaccines.

Detoxification is medicinal.

Exercise is medicinal.

Fasting is medicinal.

Laughter is medicinal.

Vegetables and fruits are medicinal.

Sleep is medicinal.

Sunlight is medicinal.

Friends are medicinal.

Digital detox is medicinal.

Prioritize them all!

What you tell yourself everyday will either build you up or break you down. Stop overthinking as it is just a waste of human energy. Trust your intuition and then make a decision. Gain experience and realize that there is nothing as perfect. Perfection is an illusion, instead choose to take action.

Remember, your mind is always eavesdropping on your self-talk, because your brain is like a supercomputer and your self-talk is the program it will run.

Audit your inner voice and stand guard to the doors of your mind, especially to the low opinions of others. And you know what; consciously make happiness your priority – Your happiness, your choice

The definition of both happiness and success is very individualistic. Different people give different definitions to what happiness means to them. But I have realized in this short life that whatever your individual definition of happiness is or even if you don't have one but still if you can figure out what gives you joy, that act, you should do more of that. If meeting a particular person lights up your day and you feel heard, seen & valued, do meet them more often. An aerobics class, a bhangra class or a simple stroll with a friend in park (or maybe all by yourself) if it gives you joy and happiness, make efforts to keep such activities in your daily routine.

I read a very beautiful line on a plank; 'Happiness is a state of mind – it's never in your circumstances.' We choose to be happy every day, every time. It's purely a choice. I always believe, the way you picture yourself can affect your happiness. So always picture yourself as a valuable, deserving and beautiful person.

'What you feed your mind becomes your reality. So feed it hope, love and faith.'

If I look at my life, there were days in fact months when I didn't feel that happiness even exists anywhere in my life. As I shared earlier, Post partum depression had hit me hard after both my kids. I didn't feel that anything can give me happiness anymore. But I tell you what, as they say having knowledge about your stars (greh), helps you sail through your bad times patiently and quietly, same way being a psychologist guided me, as I kept on trying ways which could help me probably, pushing myself every time to move out of my comforting sad mood. Moreover, when I used to push myself and come out of my comfort zone, I used to get in a position of helping someone in need. Helping others used to give me a lot of joy and it actually used to make me feel alive again. I realized that helping someone deal with their struggles helped me move out of my challenging struggling times. My younger one was born in 2020 during lockdown because of covid-19. Professionally I had taken a break (didn't have much choice). So helping someone emotionally – how? I used to find small acts of kindness on daily basis, used to make a point to talk to one who needs to be heard, the one who just want to tell someone that 'I am not well, I am facing hard times, I am finding it's hard to manage life.' Lending my ear to them and helping them wherever I could, used to make both of us feel better. Slowly I started my work online; I just used to take counseling sessions, no matter whether they were able to pay the fees or not, I was committed to be there, listening to them, helping wherever I could, as many a times I could relate to them more now as I myself had suffered emotionally.

So my dear friends, do pay attention to your happiness quotient and make efforts to keep it up. Because happiness is not the end goal, it's the journey. It's not chasing the rainbow but actually it's the rainbow itself. Figure out your own ways of happiness that is long lasting and is in your total control. Don't give your emotional control in the hands of ones who don't know how to operate sensitively.

"Whatever you hold in your mind on a consistent basis is exactly what you will experience in your life."
- Tony Robbins

16.

Staying Fit not for fashion but for better future

"Your health is an investment, not an expense."

Since childhood one phrase we keep on listening and using in school essays & college write up's is 'Health is Wealth'. But we actually come in terms with the real meaning of this phrase when we start losing the health we were blessed with. I have realized that good health is the most "for granted" of all virtues till we lose it. After having my daughters with a c-section, I kind of had a major toll on my physical self. During the first one I gained whooping 32 Kg's and for some time lost my whole self. But as being in my early 30's I still had that determination and will-power to work hard to lose that alarming number and I did it! But after 7 years of gap when I had my second daughter and woke up to the fact that the world was in shock and despair because of a major pandemic and me and my loved ones are majorly affected. Ohh, losing weight never crossed my mind and by the time I got back my sense to it, I was again 30 Kg's up!! And I tell you at 40, a woman's body becomes as stubborn as her mind!

Then came the self-curated plan to get my fitness back. This time it was not only the physical weight which needed to shed but I also had my mental baggage that was crying for help and needed to be unloaded. To tell you the fact, I was really very heavy; physically & mentally!! As a psychologist myself, helping so many people for years, I knew I myself was suffering from post-partum depression. My daughter being born in 2020, I took a break from work and the housework with one older kid and a newly born was too much to handle. The support system was majorly missing from life in this phase. Anyhow, as the song by **Billy Ocean** goes;

"When the going gets Tough, the Tough gets going."

I gathered myself, began the required work to feel lighter and fitter. Gradually, I reached my desired goal happily and at peace with myself.

"Fitness is not about being better than someone else.
It's about being better than you used to be."
– Khloe Kardashian

But one thing became crystal clear, that literally health is wealth and it's an ongoing process to stay on track. Staying fit not to 'fit' in some societal norms but to feel better about yourself, feel renewed, feel joyous and so much more. Guys, take care of this asset called 'Health' because ones you lose it, the probability to gain bigger, better things further also losses.

"Take care of your body. It's the only place you have to live."

– Jim Rohn

Hold on to this easily taken for granted blessing and work towards maintaining it early in your life. Try and eat healthy most of the times ;), track your step counts on daily basis and keep your thoughts flowing. What do I mean when I say keep your thoughts flowing? It's a reality that our thoughts can't stay static & positive at all the times. With years of practice and research, I have realized that you just need to direct them, replace them and never let them stick with you. If they get stuck, they become strong and as they get strong they make your growth stagnant. Share your troubling thoughts with someone, no matter you have a friend or family but do release your stuck thoughts as soon as possible even you can do that to a stranger. But just get rid of them.

Physical health is incomplete without mental health.

"To keep the body in good health is a duty, otherwise we shall not be able to keep our mind strong and clear."

–Buddha

Here's a gentle reminder that your mind is an organ of your body only! You can't achieve full potential and a complete definition of health, without both being in sync and perfect coordination. And also, that your heart is a powerful muscle and so should be exercised regularly as well. Love often and love deeply.

Thus, in crux, developing healthy habits is a key to a vibrant life and holistic health should be our aim. A healthy outside is an outcome of healthy inside.

"Fitness is not a destination, it's a journey."
"Make efforts to provide nourishment to all – mind, body and soul!"

17.

Maintain Mental Balance – Creating Serenity

Anything that costs you your peace,
Is very expensive!!

Reaching at this state of mind and stage of life, when you realize that mental peace and serenity are most difficult to achieve but most important to attain. It almost feels like that we don't want to mess up with our mental health and we start gauging things and situations from that perspective only.

"Balance is the key to everything. What we do, think, say, eat, feel, they all require awareness, and through this awareness, we can grow."

– Koi Fresco

Yes, it's completely true but for a beginner balance is a very heavy word in itself. In the quest to balance things in life we eventually feel we have actually lost our mental balance somewhere along the way. I like the word 'harmony' which creates the same feeling of 'trans' as 'balance'. Creating and looking for harmony between different aspects of life is what works well. But you know, what is the biggest enemy of this harmony/balance? It's the effort to achieve it all at one time.

In all these years and going through different phases of life, I have learnt that 'don't try to micro – manage things in life.' Micro-management takes away life from acts. It takes away the joy of that particular activity or work. Instead practicing mindfulness in every area of life lead to conscious decisions, brought calmness of mind and hence better mental stability. I started owning my inner peace and happiness and felt the onus for my mental health is in my own hands.

Prioritizing your life, recognizing what needs to be taken up at first and then doing it. I like the punch line of many women coaches today 'we can have it all'. Yes, I too believe that we can have it all but not at the same time! Your priority list should be maintained and updated on weekly basis, if daily monitoring is not possible.

Trying to do too many things at one time, actually creates chaos and hence many a times mental fog, anxiety and much more. It actually plays with our mental health and small disappointments harm us more. When things do not go our way, I have observed that at that particular time, we don't put enough effort to sit with that disappointment and get over with those disturbing emotions. I believe and always practiced that we need to sit, spend some time to get over with a disturbing thought or event in our life and then move to the next important issue. Staying in and moving around with some emotional baggage make things worse and eventually leads to a lot of mental and physical issues.

In my viewpoint, **Bruce Lee** gave a complete definition on how to attain serenity when he said following lines;

"You will continue to suffer if you have an emotional reaction to everything that is said to you. The power is sitting back and observing everything with logic. If words control you that means everyone else can control you. Breath and allow things to pass."

I just feel like adding here that mental serenity many a times come easily with this trick, and it is giving other people some ***'benefit of doubt'***. For example, that maybe when someone said something rude and mean it's because they are going through tough times in their own life, and you are not the reason. I believe by giving people benefit of doubt, we give ourselves peace in return. Empathizing and being non-judgmental here helps a lot.

So don't always rush things and in fact slow down at times when you need to pause and reflect. This small change in the way you handle your disappointments actually help you become such an emotionally mature person that you become a pro' in handling your emotions and you feel in-charge of them.

"Breaks aren't a nice-to-have luxury, they're a biological necessity."

Taking regular breaks is crucial for creating a sense of balance, a sense of calm and to get recharged to again start giving yourself completely to your desired chosen field. Taking care of your mental health is an act of self-love.

"Your brain works better if it's given time to decompress. Honoring your breaks lowers your stress in the short term and can fuel your productivity in the long term."

Dr. Aditi Nerukar

Disconnecting from regular routine is sometimes normal when you are growing. It's really a great thing to do because then you are becoming more closely connected to yourself.

Then to create mental balance or calmness, it's almost mandatory to learn to forgive and move on! **You need to leave what's no more serving you. Mentally, physically & spiritually – it can be your thoughts, things or people.**

'Mental balance is not a destination. In fact, it is a lifelong journey where small steps taken on daily basis lead to big progress and helps you feel stronger and recharged.'

18.

Heal from what has Hurt you

'Don't look back; you are not going that way.'

You can learn from your past, but you need to only live in 'NOW' if you want to create a legacy for tomorrow.

At last, life is life! Things happen, they are hurtful at times and thus there is need to be healed from them, so they don't create havoc. Let go off dreams/plans which didn't work and create room for new plans/dreams.

That's why; Heal from what has hurt you -

'Healing doesn't mean that the damage never existed. It simply means that the Damage no longer controls our life.'

One thing which we all should try to develop in our personalities as soon as possible is that 'things not always go as planned' and that's a big harsh truth about life. As said previously in this book that we should all plan our lives and that remains true! There is difference between letting go and giving up. Don't give up on your dreams/ plans just because of the fear that what if they at one point in our life start playing with our minds. We all need to plan our lives and plan it well but don't attach yourself too much with that plan or that vision that you lose sight of the fact that it was just a plan or a dream. If we achieve it, time to celebrate but even if it doesn't happen according to the designed plan still celebrate because we can dream again but now, we will start as an experienced enriched human and surely you will get or do something better. Don't hold on to hurtful feelings, incidents, and people. For instance, a constant issue from time immemorial is 'break up syndrome'. It was there during your parents' time, during my time and now in your time as well. But this fact also remains constant that you can always lay hands on a better person from such a large capable population of the world. No matter how much it hurts now, someday you will look back and realize your struggle changed your life for better.

They say, both hell and heaven are prevalent in this world itself. Don't let hurt make your life a living hell. Instead let hurt make you experience a heavenly life enriched with life lessons, charm and wisdom that you have gained.

"Things which matter most must never be at the mercy of things which matter least."
– Johann Wolfgang von Goethe

Learn to give yourself and others around some grace and some time. We tend to beat around the bush and also nagging ourselves for things which were at times out of our control. So it's absolutely essential to bestow some grace and shower some love on yourself on daily basis. You need to keep your cup full in order to offer some to others.

Life gets better when you give yourself the same love and kindness and grace that you are seeking from others around you.

19.

Work on Self – Growth & Self-Improvement – Staying a Learner throughout life

> ***"Live as if you were to die tomorrow. Learn as if you were to live forever."***
>
> ***– Mahatma Gandhi***

The moment we feel that we know everything even about our subject of expertise, our downfall begins. There is always something which you don't know, the new research, the new connections, the new collaborations which lead to new facts and figures. Finding joy in learning something new, keeps you renewed.

'Learning is a lifelong process.'

I am working in the field of psychology from more than 15 years, but I genuinely make efforts to learn something new whenever I get an opportunity. I love to be on the stage and imparting knowledge in my own small way but at the same time I love to be a part of the audience and in being an active listener & participant. Every person, every interaction teaches you something but for that you need to create space in your head and welcome newness. As flowing water gives us freshness and health and stagnant water breeds smell and mosquitoes, same way our thoughts and information need to be flowing to stay relevant and fresh.

'Many people keep on focusing that grass is greener somewhere else, but the fact is that grass is green where we water it!

So always remember to water your own grass instead of wasting time on gazing someone else's grass!!'

When you make efforts to improve yourself, you are actually giving yourself respect and you are honoring your needs. Doing a new course to upgrade yourself, learning a new hobby that can give you happiness or in fact pursuing an old hobby are all important for growth and empowerment. Self-care and self- love are roots of self-growth.

"Self-care is not selfish. You cannot serve from an empty vessel."

– Eleanor Brownn

Every day I spend an hour in learning something new. That new can be something from my field or something completely different skill may be music, calligraphy or dance. This helps me feel like a student and therefore feel young.

"One hour per day of study in your chosen field is all it takes.

One hour per day of study will put you at the top of your field within three years.

Within five years you'll be a national authority. In seven years, you can be one of the best people in the world at what you."

– Earl Nightingale

20.

Nurture Relationships – they Pay Back in most Unexpected times

"We've got this gift of love, but love is like a precious plant. You can't just accept it and leave it in cupboard or just think it's going to get on by itself. You've got to keep watering it. You've got to really look after it and nurture it."

– John Lennon

Ahh ... relationships – the most difficult aspect of one's life to come in terms with! But I should definitely add here that if cracked right, the most fulfilling aspect of life is our 'relationships'.

Let me explain this close to my heart topic – relationships! In my 40's, today I feel richer with some most amazing relations (though handful) I nurtured through these years. Whenever my 12-year-old asks me about friendships and gets disturbed by so called "BFF's" not acting the way they are supposed to be – I always tell her one thing, 'don't force relations, nurture them'! If they are true, they stay with you and if not, they will automatically leave you. You just need to create that air around you, which is made up of kindness, helpfulness and most important freeness! The relations which make you feel bounded, are made to be broken as no one likes to be in shackles. Relations need to be free flowing but certainly need to be taken care off. You can't think that in lieu of giving 'space' in relationships, you just were not present and approachable. There is a very fine line between giving required space in relation and being absent at the time of need.

'Don't let your differences be unresolved. You can ease the crease but it never turns out the same way.'

Relationships with the most "for granted' people of the world –parents, is utmost to be taken care off. Don't wait that when all things will fall in place then you will catch up with them, stay connected and present in their lives – they need you as all these years before you got busy in your own life, your life was their life!! So don't just elope from their lives all of a sudden. 'Parents don't need our tears when they die. They need our hugs, laughter, love and care while still alive.'

Nurturing relationships take time, efforts, and a BIG HEART. You just need to analyze the importance of a particular relation in your life and creating healthy boundaries around it. Then don't let small issues take over your love. Never keep relations under constant scrutiny and fear of losing. Relationships are a lot of investment – here I am talking about emotional investment, so be careful before investing but not be fearful. Be genuine and relaxed because whenever you are too eager to get in a relationship, you end up feeling emotionally drained. So never be pushy, or forceful.

Today we are surrounded by the fear of commitment and thus trust in relations is majorly missing. One is not ready to commit, and the other is not ready to trust. The new concept in relationships for example, 'Situationship' emphasize this only – the fear to take the next step and commit! That's why I believe, let love be love, marriage be marriage and friends be friends. Mixing relationships can only mess up your feelings and hence your life.

Every healthy relationship whether personal or professional demands respect, space and an open communication. Learning where to give space and where to exert your power of friendship is what you need to learn. Beautiful relationships need time, trust and tons of love & care.

But definitely look for red flags in relationships – whether looking for spouse or friends.

- Creating boundaries not boundations!
- Prioritize self-respect but not false ego!
- Value yourself but empathize with others!

"The worst thing in life is to end up with people that make you feel all alone."

– Robin Williams

21.

Add Value to people's life – your Presence should always be One plus One equals to Eleven

"Adding value to others is the surest way to add value to our own lives."

– John C. Maxwell

Mantra to become 'Irreplaceable' is adding value. When I was young, I used to observe my mom getting involved with the host, helping them serve, making them clean after party and so on – I always used to wonder why she has to go overboard. But as I grew and after many open discussions with her, I understood this beautiful philosophy of adding value. She explained to me that I don't believe in exerting oneself to a level of exhaustion but being genuinely around and offering support whenever someone needs it is the mantra. This habit of her always used to make a go to person at parties and in fact at her workplace as well. She was genuinely approachable. One point she always added that gauge carefully, whether the person in front is going to be respectful of your being an asset to them and if not then always maintain a distance. Then learn to say No when and where you can be available and don't over stretch yourself. **Learning to say 'No'** is a part of respecting yourself and never let anyone take you for granted.

> ***"Strive not to be a success,***
> ***but rather to be of value."***
>
> ***– Albert Einstein***

Everyone is doing their assigned KRA's but doing that extra gesture of may be helping in organizing an office party, of taking up stage responsibility, organizing games, helping someone manage their extra load for just 10 minutes a day, taking some responsibility at religious place or community center etc. are adding extra value. Without being exploited, you can do a lot for adding value to other people's life and some nice accolades to your name!

> ***'To inspire people, don't show them your superpower. Show them theirs!'***